CW00742924

AARDMAN

Wallace & Gromit™

VENGEANCE MOST FOWL

First published 2024 by Macmillan Children's Books
an imprint of Pan Macmillan
The Smithson, 6 Briset Street, London, EC1M 5NR
EU representative: Macmillan Publishers Ireland Limited, 1st Floor,
The Liffey Trust Centre,
117–126 Sheriff Street Upper, Dublin 1, D01 YC43

Associated companies throughout the world
www.panmacmillan.com

ISBN: 978-1-0350-2322-6

Written by Amanda Li
Based on the film *Wallace & Gromit: Vengeance Most Fowl*

1 3 5 7 9 8 6 4 2

A CIP catalogue record for this book is available from the British Library.

Printed and bound by CPI Group (UK) Ltd

AARDMAN

Wallace & Gromit™

VENGEANCE MOST FOWL

THE JUNIOR NOVEL

MACMILLAN CHILDREN'S BOOKS

CHAPTER ONE

THE CAPTURE OF THE CENTURY

A thunderstorm raged outside 62 West Wallaby Street, the home of Wallace and his faithful dog, Gromit.

FLASH! Lightning lit up the window, revealing a small dark figure tied to a chair in the kitchen. He sat very still, staring straight ahead with black beady eyes. It was most sinister.

In the room next door, a panicky Wallace picked up the phone. Gromit watched as his master dialled 999 with trembling hands.

'Hello?' said Wallace. 'Is that the police? I think we've just foiled a robbery!'

NEE NAW, NEE NAW! In minutes, a police van, blue lights flashing, screeched to a halt outside the house. In ran the police, handcuffs at the ready. The creepy captive was arrested and driven directly to the police station.

As the van zoomed off, Wallace and Gromit looked at each other. They had done it! Together they had captured a ruthless villain. It was time

to celebrate – with a nice cup of tea, of course. Gromit made a brew, and the pair clinked their mugs together in congratulations.

But who was this mysterious villain?

It was none other than criminal mastermind, Feathers McGraw! This pesky penguin – who committed his crimes while disguised as a chicken – had stolen the priceless Blue Diamond from the town museum and tried to frame Wallace for the crime. Feathers had almost got away with it – but Wallace and Gromit had outsmarted him.

As the duo sipped their tea, Feathers arrived at the police station. He silently tossed his things into a box: a bunch of keys, a comb, a tape measure and a red rubber glove. The glove was Feathers's master stroke, his cunning disguise. Simply by placing it on his head, the penguin was transformed into a red-combed chicken. But not any longer.

Days later, the feathered felon stood in court to hear the final verdict.

'You have been found guilty of the attempted robbery of the Blue Diamond,' announced the judge. 'And if not for the actions of two upstanding citizens you would have succeeded in your wicked plan!' Those upstanding citizens were, of course, Wallace and Gromit.

There was quiet as everyone waited to hear the sentence.

'It is the decision of this court that for the rest of your natural life you be removed to a high-security institution!' boomed the judge, banging her gavel.

Feathers McGraw looked straight ahead, his

expression blank, as the guards removed him from court and took him to his new home.

It was a strange-looking place for a jail. White fake snowy humps surrounded a small swimming pool. A sign said **FEEDING TIMES**. Other signposts pointed to **BIG CATS** and the **REPTILE HOUSE**. Feathers looked carefully at his new surroundings. He was in a zoo. But this was no ordinary zoo. It was a high-security penguin enclosure with heavy iron bars across the gates. His thoughts were interrupted by the arrival of two uniformed zookeepers.

'There's no escape from here – so don't even

think about it!' said the first one, with a nasty laugh. Feathers looked at them both without blinking.

CLANG! The keepers put him in a cell connected to the penguin enclosure and slammed the door shut, glad to be away from the penguin's stony stare. Feathers McGraw was safely locked up for the rest of his life and would never get out. Now he was left alone to dwell on his fate.

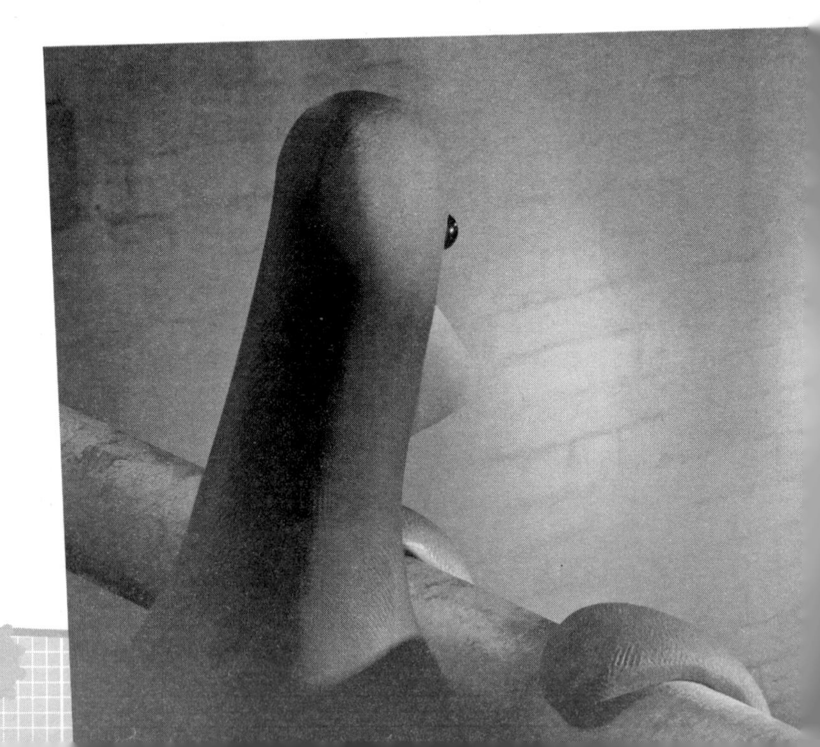

As Feathers adjusted to life in his new home, he didn't give the guards any trouble. He soon fell into a routine, doing penguin pull-ups every day to keep fit. All the while, the brooding bird gazed at the newspaper cutting he kept pinned to his cell wall.

DIAMOND GEEZERS CATCH THIEF! announced the headline. There was a photograph of a delighted Wallace and Gromit, celebrating Feathers's capture.

Feathers observed the man and dog who had foiled his cunning plan. He was in no rush. He would wait for the right time. But, come what may, he would get his revenge on the pair that had put him behind bars.

Of that he was sure.

CHAPTER TWO

TOO MANY GADGETS

Many years later, a new day was dawning at 62 West Wallaby Street.

BRRIINNGG! went Gromit's alarm clock. **WHOOSH!** The bedroom curtains opened and bright rays of sunlight hit Gromit's face. Gromit opened one sleepy eye – then pulled the covers over his head and carried on dozing.

But not for long. Another of Wallace's waking devices kicked in. **SCHLOOOP!**

This time Gromit's whole body was sucked up by a bleeping suction tube and firmly dropped into his waiting slippers. Gromit was awake! He yawned, shook out his ears and started making the morning tea.

Grabbing a mug from a dispenser, Gromit inserted it into Wallace's special tea-making machine. A gush of steaming liquid quickly filled it up. But nothing was ever simple at 62 West Wallaby Street. As Gromit raised his mug to drink, mechanical arms interrupted him, trying to stir his tea with a spoon. Gromit managed one slurp before a robot vacuum cleaner whizzed up to take his mug away. He shook his head impatiently and backed away from the over-enthusiastic gadgets.

BZZZ! At that moment, a picture of Wallace on the wall whirred into life. His eyes lit up and an attached mechanical hand started to wave at Gromit.

'Get me up, Gromit!' he said cheerfully. 'Another great day of inventing beckons!'

An obedient Gromit headed for the dining room and pulled a lever on the **GET-U-UP DELUXE**. Wallace had been tinkering with his invention and now it was new and improved.

'Top dog!' said Wallace, beaming from the monitor. The **GET-U-UP DELUXE** burst into action, as it did every morning.

Up shot Wallace's bed, tipping him forward through a hole in the floor.

'Tally ho!' he shouted with glee. Then 'Whoooa!' as his pyjamas were whisked away, and he landed with a ***PLOP!*** into a warm, foamy bath.

'Ooh, lovely,' sighed Wallace, sinking into the bubbles.

Gromit turned the dial from **SOAK** to **SCRUB** and a rotating device of sponges began to give Wallace a good washing.

'Ooh! Ha ha! That tickles!' he giggled as the spinning sponges whirred around his body. Washing completed, the naked Wallace was tipped out into a large transparent tube, which was attached to the outside wall of the house.

'Wheee!' he shouted as he whizzed through the tube, rosy and glowing from all the scrubbing.

Gromit, who had just popped outside with the bin bags, covered his eyes. Fortunately, Wallace quickly shot back inside the house. Here the **DRESS-O-MATIC** did its work, grabbing Wallace and dropping him smartly into a pair of trousers suspended from the ceiling. More mechanical arms shot out to put on Wallace's shirt and plonk a helmet on his head.

Just as Wallace was adjusting his tie – ***SPROING!*** – a mallet labelled **EXTRA BOOST** catapulted him upwards, straight into the dining room, where his helmeted head smacked a bell. ***DING!*** A bright **GOOD MORNING** sign lit up. Wallace landed in his chair with a ***WHUMP!***

Gromit was already sitting at the table, the tea made and the morning post ready. An arm shot out and removed Wallace's helmet.

'Morning, Gromit,' he said, cheerily. 'How's my favourite pooch?'

Gromit raised his eyebrows and handed his owner a new copy of *Practical Inventor*.

'You do look after me, lad,' said a grateful Wallace, taking his favourite magazine.

Gromit whipped on his sunglasses to protect his eyes as the **JAM-BALLISTER** machine suddenly whirred into action. Dollops of jam, marmalade and peanut butter were hurled through the air, some even landing on the toast. Gromit patiently wiped the sticky splodges from his shades. An automatic feeding hand shoved the jammy buttered toast into Wallace's open mouth.

'Mmm,' he said, munching away. 'Cracking toast, Gromit!' He flicked through the *Practical Inventor* while Gromit began sorting through a large pile of post. Most were envelopes stamped with red warnings: **'URGENT', 'OUTSTANDING', 'PAY NOW – OR ELSE!'**

'Oh dear,' said Wallace, noticing the envelopes. 'More bills? Inventing doesn't come cheap, does it?' He thought for a moment. 'Maybe I'm just making too many gadgets?'

He put down his magazine and looked at Gromit, who was shaking himself vigorously. He had just been showered in milk by yet another breakfast gadget.

'Don't worry, lad,' said Wallace reassuringly. 'We'll think of something.' He beckoned to Gromit. 'You look like you need a good pat. Come here.' Gromit perked up. He loved a pat! He trotted over expectantly, but, to his surprise, Wallace pressed a button.

'My new **PAT-O-MATIC** will oblige!' he said, watching his latest invention come to life. Gromit blinked in surprise as a mechanical hand suddenly appeared and began awkwardly

W

patting him on the head. Gromit frowned. This was no substitute for a human hand.

Wallace, however, was delighted. He leapt up from his chair, in excitement.

'I've got a "pat" pending on that!' he announced. 'And wait till you see the next thing I'm working on!' With that, the bald-headed inventor disappeared into the basement.

Gromit looked at the **PAT-O-MATIC** and sighed. What would Wallace get up to next?

Chapter Three

WELCOME GNOME!

After a challenging morning, Gromit needed some peace and quiet. He got out his garden tools and headed for his little piece of paradise – the back garden of West Wallaby Street. It was a lovely spot. Flowers bloomed, birds tweeted and bees buzzed as Gromit picked up his trowel and started planting. He sighed happily. A haven of peace and not a gadget in sight.

It didn't last long. Behind him, a figure came into view pushing a trolley. ***RUMBLE!***

RUMBLE! A startled Gromit turned round. There was Wallace, wheeling a tall heavy-looking crate into the garden. He came to a sudden stop.

'Phew!' said Wallace, mopping his brow. 'Don't think I haven't noticed, Gromit. You spend ages toiling away in this garden. Well, not any more!'

Gromit stared at the wooden crate in alarm. There was a loud **CRACK!** and the front burst open, making Gromit jump out of his skin. He peered in cautiously to see . . . a large friendly-looking garden gnome wearing a green jacket and red hat! Gromit was used to Wallace's surprises, but this was unlike anything he'd ever seen before.

'This is my latest invention!' said Wallace with pride. 'A Smart Gnome!'

The Smart Gnome emerged from the crate. 'Hi,' it said. 'I'm your Nifty Odd-jobbing Robot. Call me Norbot.'

'Norbot – meet Gromit,' said Wallace.

'Pleased to meet you,

Master Gromit!' said Norbot, holding out his hand. Gromit took it cautiously. Norbot shook his paw extremely hard, making Gromit jiggle up and down. There was an awkward pause.

'Well, go on,' said Wallace to Gromit. 'Put him through his little paces. He's voice-activated!' Gromit rolled his eyes, but Wallace didn't notice. 'Bit shy, are we?' he continued. He turned to his gnome. 'All right, Norbot. Make Gromit's garden neat and tidy.'

'Neat and tidy,' replied Norbot. 'Yes, Mr Wallace!' The gnome quickly scanned the garden using its Norbot-cam, then headed into Gromit's shed.

'I've pre-programmed him for you, lad!' said Wallace. 'He's watched every episode of *DIY Garden Squad*!' Norbot came out of the shed, holding a pair of garden shears.

'Only two hours to go and they still haven't got the patio down!' said Norbot, clearly a big fan of the show. Wallace smiled at him.

'Just watch him do all those tedious gardening tasks!' he said as Norbot got to work. Quick as a flash, the gnome started mowing, pruning, trimming and strimming. A shocked Gromit leapt into the air as Norbot sliced through the toes of his gardening boots. ***WHOOSH!*** Norbot blasted Gromit with a powerful leaf blower, lifting him off his feet and whirling leaves into his face.

'Chop, chop, chop,' uttered Norbot as he rushed around. 'Mowing! More mowing! Strimmer! Pointlessly blowing leaves around! Last bit of mowing!' With this, he mowed down Gromit's lovely new sapling that he had just planted.

'Neat and tidy!' said a satisfied Norbot.

Gromit surveyed his once lush, flower-filled garden in dismay. After Norbot's extreme cutting, it was reduced to a geometric green square.

There was a sudden round of applause, and he turned to see a crowd of people standing by the fence. Norbot had some admirers!

The neighbours had been watching him perform his speedy gardening tasks, and some passers-by had joined them too. Even a lorry driver had parked his truck so he could watch the Smart Gnome at work. There were cries of 'He's a little treasure!' and 'Amazing job!'

Wallace was delighted at his robot's reception. 'Looks like you've made the cut, Norbot!' he said. 'Better take a bow!' As Norbot bowed to his audience, laughter broke out and there was more clapping. Someone even threw flowers as if Norbot had just given a prize-winning performance. Gromit did a double take. Those were *his* precious flowers, grown by Gromit – and cut down by Norbot!

'Where did you get him from?' cried their neighbour, Mr Windfall.

'Actually, I made him myself,' said Wallace, blushing slightly.

'Ooh – is he for hire?' asked Mrs Windfall.

‘Is he for hire?’ repeated Wallace, thinking hard. An inspired idea came to him. He beckoned enthusiastically. ‘Come on, I need your help!’ he cried. Gromit took a step towards him. ‘No, not you, lad,’ said Wallace impatiently. ‘I meant Norbot!’

‘Yes, Mr Wallace,’ said Norbot, coming over to Wallace.

‘Come along, Norbot, lad, we’ve got work to do,’ said Wallace. He and Norbot rushed off, leaving a confused Gromit on his own. Not quite sure what to do, Gromit put on his straw gardening hat, only to find that Norbot had trimmed it down to a square.

Gromit frowned. This gnome could be bad news!

Chapter Four

THE BLUE DIAMOND IS BACK!

Down at the police station, Chief Inspector Mackintosh was in his office, holding a framed photograph of the thing he loved most in the world. 'It's a crime that you and I can't be together,' he cried, gazing at his beauty. He kissed the photo lovingly and placed it back on his desk. 'Not yet, my sweetness – but soon!' he whispered.

The photograph was of a canal boat with the name of *Dun Nickin*.

The inspector was interrupted by a knock at the door.

'Got a mo', Chief?' It was PC Mukherjee, a keen young police constable who was new to the job. She bounded into the room, holding a large pile of files. 'I've just finished my investigation into that missing bike saddle,' she announced, slamming the files on to the desk and making the inspector jump. 'I've got witness interviews, crime-scene reports, full forensics!' she said, excitedly.

'Mukherjee,' said the inspector, trying to interrupt her.

PC Mukherjee's eyes gleamed. 'AND I checked the National Bike Saddle database. Only there isn't one, apparently—'

'MUKHERJEE!' cried the inspector, pushing her file to the side. 'How long have you been with us now?'

'Since nine o'clock this morning, Chief,' said Mukherjee, standing to attention.

'Well,' said the inspector. 'You can forget what you learned at training college, Mukherjee, because at the end of the day, there's just one thing that matters in this job. A copper's gut.'

Mukherjee looked confused. The inspector got up and began to pace the room.

'Instinct,' he said, dramatically. 'The important stuff's not up here,' he said, tapping his head. 'It's down here,' he said, patting his stomach with pride. 'I've got quite a copper's gut myself, actually.'

'Oh, I can see that, Chief,' said PC Mukherjee, looking at his round belly. 'Oops – I didn't mean . . .' She quickly changed the subject. 'Is that Feathers McGraw?' she asked.

'What? Where?' blurted the inspector in a panic. Then he realized that Mukherjee was looking at an old poster on the wall and calmed

down. 'Ah, the poster.' They both stared at the photograph of the sinister penguin. He was in disguise, wearing his trademark red fingered glove on his head. The words

HAVE YOU SEEN THIS CHICKEN?

were printed above him.

'Well, there you go! A copper's gut!' said the inspector. 'I *knew* he was a wrong un.'

'He stole the Blue Diamond, right?' asked PC Mukherjee.

'Oh, he tried,' said the inspector. 'But he couldn't escape the long arm of the law.' He cast his mind back in time to when he was a police constable, just like Mukherjee. 'Oh yes,

I played my part,' he said, remembering the day of Feathers McGraw's arrest. How could he forget it? He was the policeman who had answered the panic-stricken phone call from Wallace, with the news that Feathers was captured.

After the villain had been arrested, PC Mackintosh had enjoyed all the attention – the congratulations, the press interviews, his photograph in the newspapers. He became ambitious and vowed to rise to the top of his profession. Now here he was, a chief inspector nearing retirement.

'The Blue Diamond ended up back in the museum vault,' said the inspector. 'I locked it up myself. Well out of harm's way.'

PC Mukherjee was impressed. 'Ooh, I'd love to crack a case like that,' she said. 'You must be dead proud, Chief!'

'It's not about pride, Mukherjee,' he replied. 'It's about duty. Which is why I've accepted one last task before I hang up my truncheon.' Chief Inspector Mackintosh moved aside his boat photo to reveal a set of plans on his desk.

'It's the new Blue Diamond Exhibition!' he

announced. Mukherjee's mouth dropped open.

'The diamond's going back on display?' she cried.

'Oh, aye,' said the inspector. 'I've designed all the security arrangements myself. It's foolproof.'

Mukherjee looked at the plans more closely. 'Hmm,' she said, taking in the details. 'What if Feathers cuts a hole in that skylight?'

'Skylight?' said the inspector, nervously.

'Or if he removes the back plate off the air con?' continued Mukherjee. 'Or he could just get in through the gift shop.'

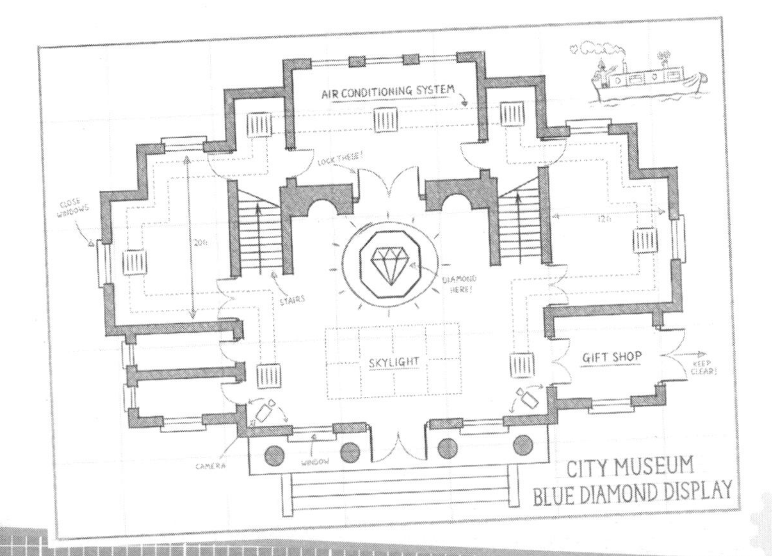

‘There’s a gift shop?’ said the inspector, beginning to panic. He’d had enough of this. He grabbed the plans and rolled them up, away from Mukherjee’s eagle eyes.

‘Look, Feathers isn’t going to get in,’ he said, crossly. ‘He’s safely banged up in the zoo. Literally doing bird. Now, I’ve got a Grand Opening to prepare for. So get out there on the beat. Burn some shoe leather!’

‘YES!’ Mukherjee exclaimed, excited to be going on duty. She collected herself. ‘I mean, *yes, sir.*’

With that, the inspector ushered Mukherjee out of his office and slammed the door with a ‘Hrmph!’

CHAPTER FIVE

NO PLACE LIKE GNOME

Norbot was having a very busy day. He was standing on a ladder with a brush, painting a sign on a brand-new van. It was the latest in a long list of jobs he'd been doing for Wallace.

'That's it, Norbot!' said Wallace. 'Make the letters nice and big.'

A puzzled Gromit was watching from the

sidelines, wondering what was going on. Norbot stepped back from his painting to reveal the van's brand-new logo.

GNOME IMPROVEMENTS – NO JOB TOO SMALL

'Da na!' cried Wallace.

'Da na!' said Norbot, copying him.

'You see, Gromit?' said Wallace, proudly. '*Gnome Improvements* – a gnome-based garden and maintenance service. I told you we'd find a way to pay the bills, lad.' Gromit brightened up. A new business? Maybe this was a good idea?

Wallace looked at the van again. 'Norbot – haven't you missed something?' he said. Straight away, Norbot painted on some extra letters. He stepped back. The sign now read:

WALLACE AND NORBOT'S
GNOME IMPROVEMENTS

'Good job, Norbot!' said Wallace, with a smile. Gromit's face fell. With Norbot around, he was beginning to feel left out.

At that moment, a truck pulled up with a ***HONK HONK!*** It was Up North News, the local TV news service. The truck door opened and out jumped local reporter Onya Doorstep, closely followed by a camera operator.

'Ooh, this will be great for publicity,' said Wallace, excitedly. He adjusted his tie. 'Look smart, Norbot – and let me do the talking.' He rushed off to greet Onya.

'Let you do the talking,' said Norbot, also adjusting his tie. 'Yes, Mr Wallace.' He tossed away his paint-stained rag and followed Wallace. The rag hit Gromit full in the face.

Gromit threw it on the ground and glared at Norbot's retreating figure.

❁❁❁

Later that evening, Wallace and Norbot settled themselves down on the comfy sofa. Gromit was sitting on his own, but Wallace didn't notice. He turned on the TV excitedly, just in time for the evening news. It was introduced in the studio by presenter, Anton Deck.

'Good evening,' said Anton, with a big smile. 'Now, we've all heard of cutting-edge technology but how about "cutting hedge" technology? Ha ha! Over to Onya Doorstep for more!'

Onya Doorstep appeared on screen, standing by the *Gnome Improvement* van. Next to her was Norbot.

'Meet Norbot,' she said. 'The latest thing in "Gnome Help". He's the brainchild of a smart-thinking local inventor.'

'Smart thinking!' said a pleased Wallace, from the sofa. 'Thank you very much!' Wallace's face then loomed on to the TV screen. He looked rather nervous.

'So, Wallace,' said Onya, offering him the microphone, 'what can Norbot do around the house?'

'Oh, well, pretty much everything, Ms Doorstep,' said Wallace, rather awkwardly. He wasn't used to being on the telly.

'No job is too small!' said Norbot. In seconds, he had clipped a large bush into an impressive figure to demonstrate his skills. An annoyed Gromit brushed the falling leaves from his head.

'I've been testing him out here in my garden and he's done a cracking job, as you can see,' said Wallace, pointing at the lawn.

'He certainly seems very user-friendly,' said Onya. 'So – what inspired you to create this handy device, Mr Wallace?'

'Oh,' said Wallace, modestly. 'I've always loved inventing. Making things that help people. I'd say Norbot's my greatest invention so far. We charge him up overnight and the next day he's raring to go again!'

'He seems very obliging,' said Onya.

'Whatever your problem – he's the answer,' replied Wallace, forgetting his nerves.

'Well, it sounds like this little gnome is going to make a huge difference around here!' said Onya. She looked at the camera to finish her report. 'This is Onya Doorstep for *Up North News*.'

From the sofa, Wallace let out a delighted cry. 'A.I., lad!' he said, getting up to put on the tea-making machine. 'See how embracing technology makes our life better!' Gromit was

busy knitting Wallace a pair of socks and didn't bother to look up.

'I mean, thanks to this handy device, we haven't had to use the old teapot for years,' said Wallace. He watched with satisfaction as his gadget poured the tea, stirred the tea and tapped the spoon against the cup. Gromit looked sadly at the old teapot on the shelf, gathering dust.

'Tech,' said Wallace, nodding. 'That's the thing. So long as it knows who's boss, of course.'

Gromit felt a sudden yank on his knitting. He looked up to see his ball of wool spinning madly. Norbot was also knitting, his needles clacking away furiously. In seconds, the gnome had produced a complete trouser/tank-top/shirt onesie. He had also used up all of Gromit's wool.

'Da na!' said Norbot, handing the knitted outfit to Wallace.

'Ooh, a Wallace onesie!' said Wallace, holding it up to himself. 'That's champion, that is, Norbot!'

Gromit put down his half-knitted sock and frowned. This was all getting too much.

Chapter Six

NORBOT IN THE NEWS

In the penguin enclosure, Feathers McGraw had been listening to the very same news report. Banged up in his cell, he poked a shiny sardine tin through his food flap to get a better view of the zookeepers' TV. What he saw in the tin's reflection was very interesting indeed.

Feathers recognized Wallace – the bald-headed idiot in a tank top who had got him put away. But, strangely, his canine companion was nowhere to be seen. Wallace had a new friend by the name of Norbot. And Norbot was a Smart Gnome.

Feathers's evil mind whirred as he realized that a delicious opportunity had just presented itself. But his thoughts were interrupted by the clinking sound of keys in the door. It was the zookeepers doing their nightly check. Feathers quickly slipped the sardine mirror out of the food flap and hid it away.

'Move aside, jailbird!' said a voice. Feathers sat silently on his bed as two keepers came in and inspected his cell. A pair of red rubber gloves hung from one of their belts and Feathers's beady eyes glinted. As always, he saw everything, but said nothing.

'All clear,' called the zookeepers, slamming the door. 'Don't know why everyone thinks he so's clever,' said one as they disappeared down the corridor.

Feathers stayed still for a moment. Then he held up a red rubber glove that he'd just stolen from the guard. He stretched it out and snapped it back in satisfaction.

Feathers was back in business.

Darkness fell and the occupants of 62 West Wallaby Street drank their nightly cocoa. Gromit badly needed some 'me-time' after his difficult day with Norbot. He got into bed, turned on his radio and opened his book with a contented sigh. Relaxing music filled the room.

He didn't hear the bedroom door creak open and the sound of footsteps padding towards him.

'Evening, Master Gromit!' came a familiar voice. Gromit looked up and groaned. Not Norbot again! At that moment the calming music stopped.

Huh? thought Gromit, looking at his radio. The plug was lying on the floor. Norbot had pulled it out of the socket and plugged in his own charger!

'Norbot recharge time!' announced Norbot. A loud humming sound filled the air as the gnome settled down to charge himself. It was very irritating.

Gromit's peace was ruined. He closed his

book with an angry **SNAP!** and turned off the light, giving Norbot a furious look. Then he got under the covers and settled down to try to get some sleep.

Moments later – **CLICK!** Norbot's eyes lit up like two bright torches in the dark. With the light in his eyes, Gromit tossed and turned, unable to sleep. The loud humming continued, torturing his ears.

'**RECHARGE** – nearly one per cent!' blared out Norbot. That was it! An angry Gromit jumped out of bed and grabbed the noisy gnome. He marched down the stairs into the basement – the furthest place from his bedroom – and looked for a spare plug socket. Every socket was taken up with one of Wallace's many devices. Gromit spotted Wallace's computer and plugged Norbot into its side.

'Recharge time re-activated,' said Norbot. Gromit left him to it and stomped up the steps.

'Recharge nearly two per cent,' uttered Norbot from below. Gromit slammed the basement door and stormed upstairs to his room. Finally, he might get some sleep!

Chapter Seven

A HEARTLESS HACKER

The moment he had spotted Wallace's Smart Gnome on the news, Feathers's brain had gone into overdrive. It wasn't long before he had masterminded a complicated plan. It would be his most devious and slippery scheme yet!

The crafty penguin had been collecting selected bits of junk for months. He emptied them out on to a crate, then got to work by candlelight. Using lolly sticks, bottle caps, rubber bands and an old skipping rope he had soon assembled an ingenious extendable 'arm'. At the end of the arm, he attached the stolen red rubber glove.

Feathers stood on tiptoe and ripped the newspaper cutting of Wallace and Gromit from his cell wall. Behind it was a loose brick.

Feathers pulled the brick out and peered through the gap into the corridor. The coast was clear. He took the extendable arm and fed it through the hole, operating it slowly and skilfully.

The zookeeper was snoring away at the guard station. She didn't see the arm moving behind her, edging towards the keys hanging from the hook. But what was this? The arm slid

past the keys, towards the computer keyboard on the desk. It seemed that Feathers wasn't planning to escape just yet.

From his cell, the penguin adjusted the arm so that the gloved hand found the keyboard. Then he began tapping out a series of complicated letters and numbers. Hc checked the code by peering through a telescope made from a round tube of sweets.

Feathers was hacking into a computer. A computer that was located in the basement of 62 West Wallaby Street!

A stray feather drifted on to the zookeeper's nose. She stirred in her sleep and took a sudden breath, about to sneeze. Feathers quickly whipped the gloved hand to her nose, stopping the sneeze with a well-placed finger. Beads of sweat ran down his beak. But another sneeze was coming, even bigger this time.

'Aaah, aaah, aaah, ***CHOO!***' spluttered the guard. The gloved hand pulled a hanky out of her top pocket and caught it, just in time. Feathers wiped the sweat away, then got back to work.

Soon he had found the document he wanted, named: **WALLACE'S FILES**. But there was a problem.

The screen flashed up: **ENTRY DENIED**. Feathers paused. He needed Wallace's password. The brainy bird put himself in Wallace's shoes and tapped in an intelligent guess:

First try: **GROM1TDOG**

Then: **1NV3NTOR**

No luck. A warning message flashed up – **ONE ATTEMPT LEFT.** Feathers tapped his chin thoughtfully. This was proving tricky. He looked around and noticed the guard's newspaper cutting of Wallace and Gromit on the wall. In the photo, Wallace was celebrating his success with his all-time favourite snack: crackers and cheese. That was it! Feathers tapped in:

C-H-E-E-S-E

Success!

Next a page of random pictures appeared. The instruction **SELECT ALL SQUARES WITH CHEESE** came up. Feathers blinked in frustration. What was this?

He carefully selected two pictures of cheese. Then he paused at a picture of the moon. Was it made of cheese? He pondered for a moment then clicked on the image. Yes!

He was in!

The gloved hand clicked on a folder named **NORBOT**, which immediately revealed pages of technical specs for Wallace's Smart Gnome design. Feathers clicked on **SETTINGS** and soon found **CORE PROTOCOL**.

The setting was on **GOOD**. The penguin quickly scrolled through the other options: pleasant, unassuming, dull, bit selfish, grumpy, really nasty – and finally: **EVIL**. That was the one!

The feathered fiend selected it triumphantly. His job was done!

In seconds, the arm was withdrawn, the brick replaced and the newspaper cutting stuck back on the wall. Everything looked exactly as before. Feathers lay back on his cell bed, relaxed and satisfied with his night's work.

In the dark basement of West Wallaby Street, Norbot had almost finished charging from Wallace's computer. His eyes suddenly lit up as a new command came down the line. He twitched horribly as Feathers's dreadful data flowed into his operating system.

'New instructions received!' said Norbot with a horrible grin . He picked up Wallace's power tools and crossed over to the work bench where the Smart Gnome's blueprints were displayed. He looked at the plans and switched on the power tools with a **SCREECH!**

The new evil Norbot was about to start work.

Chapter Eight

A Number of Norbots

The next morning, Gromit went through his usual routine, finishing off with cereal served by Wallace's breakfast dispenser. He had just opened a book to read when the

GET-U-UP DELUXE intercom buzzed. Wallace's voice came through loud and clear.

'Get me up, lad! We've got a right busy day ahead!' he cried. Gromit sighed, put down his book and gave the **GET-U-UP** lever a tug. 'Tally ho!' shouted Wallace as he was tipped from his bed into the slippery chute.

CLOMP! CLOMP! Gromit's ears twitched at the sound of Norbot's footsteps coming down the hallway. Today they sounded different somehow. Gromit looked up as Norbot entered the room. There was definitely something strange about him.

Norbot turned – and stared at Gromit with cold, deadly eyes. Gromit's eyes widened in shock. ***PLOMP!*** Wallace appeared, dropping into his chair at the table.

'Morning, team!' he said, cheerily. He slurped his tea loudly, then checked the answerphone.

'Loads of new messages!' he said, pressing a button to hear them. Various voices could be heard, all of them villagers wanting Norbot to do jobs for them.

'Talk about celebrity – he's a "household gnome"!' said Wallace, happily. 'At this rate, we'll need a whole army of Norbots!'

Norbot, who had been silent up until now, raised his hands and gave a loud **CLAP!** Out of nowhere, the room began to vibrate and everything on the table rattled. Deep rumbles could be felt from the ground below them.

'Eh?' said a confused Wallace. Gromit frowned and went downstairs to see what the commotion was. He opened the basement door, peering into the darkness. There was a sudden

CLOMP! CLOMP! CLOMP! of footsteps. A shocked Gromit leapt out of the way as a whole procession of Norbots came marching up the steps!

The gnomes trooped out of the basement and lined up in the hallway like an army regiment. How had this happened? Numerous numbers of Norbots! Gromit shook his head in disbelief. Somehow, Norbot had gone and replicated himself! The only difference was that they were dressed in blue!

Wallace appeared and saw all the gnomes. 'What on earth . . .?' he uttered, his mouth open in amazement.

'More Norbots for Mr Wallace,' said the original Norbot.

'Well,' said Wallace, looking impressed. 'That IS smart. It's like he knows what we need before we even know ourselves!'

Gromit stared at the Norbot army. He didn't

like the look of them at all. Wallace, meanwhile, was checking out the gnome line-up.

'The more gnomes, the merrier. Right, Gromit?' he said. All the Norbot army saluted him.

'The more gnomes, the merrier,' said the original Norbot.

'YES, MR WALLACE,' chorused the Norbot army.

'Ha ha!' laughed Wallace. 'What could go wrong?' Gromit raised an eyebrow. He'd heard it all before.

Wallace began organizing the gnomes straight away. The original Norbot would drive all the gnomes to the village in the van, then each gnome would travel by moped to a different customer. With his army of gnomes, all their jobs would be done in a jiffy!

Gromit made tea as Wallace set up a radar

dish on the roof to help him track the Norbot army. Then he positioned himself in the back room – now his control room – surrounded by flickering CCTV screens and keyboards.

'I just track them with my new Gnoming Device,' said Wallace, watching on screen as the gnomes piled into the van. Gromit came in with a tray of mugs. 'No need for us to go with them, Gromit!'

Gromit looked at the screen, frowning. He didn't trust those gnomes. Someone needed to go along and keep an eye on them.

'Lovely tea,' said Wallace, slurping. 'Now, all we have to do is sit back and let the machines take the strain, right, Gromit?' He looked round. 'Gromit?'

Gromit was gone.

VROOM VROOM! Wallace heard the van revving and jumped out of his chair. 'Gromit!' he called. But Gromit had taken the van keys and forced the original Norbot out of the driver's seat. Now he was at the wheel, about to drive off with all the gnomes.

Inside the van, Wallace's crackly voice came over the intercom. 'I said we don't need to go with them. Don't you trust my inventions, lad?' Gromit looked round at the army of Norbots behind him. He didn't trust any of them, not one little gnomy bit.

He drove on, a determined look on his face.

CHAPTER NINE

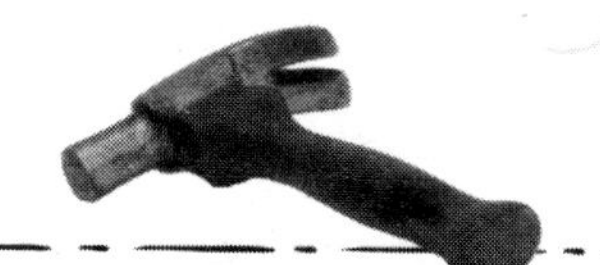

THE NORBOT ARMY GET BUSY

Back at the house, Wallace shook his head. 'That dog!' he said, tutting to himself. He turned back to his screens to check the van's progress. It had now arrived at its destination. 'Time to unleash the gnomes!' said Wallace, pressing lots of buttons.

The back door of the van opened and the Norbot army whizzed out on speedy little scooters. 'Go! Go! Go!' shouted the original Norbot as the gnomes sped towards their customers.

'Remember, I want you all working like a finely tuned machine,' came Wallace's voice over the intercom. He watched their progress on the Gnome Tracker screen in delight.

The Norbot army spread out around the town and found their customers. In no time, they were doing tasks, jobs and chores for delighted villagers. What a team they were! The gnomes worked together like clockwork, trimming lawns, painting houses and sawing wood.

As they worked, they danced and sang:

'Oh, we're happy nifty Norbots!
We love to do a job!
When we come round and fix your
house, we make up quite a mob.
We dig and paint and plant and snip–
We'll break our little backs–
And never stop to have a brew,
'Cause we got battery packs!

Oh, we're jolly useful Norbots!
We do all sorts of stuff!
When we get asked to do a task, we
can't work hard enough!
We push and pull and saw and chop–
We think our chores are fun–
We won't delay, keep out our way,
Until the job is done!'

The villagers loved the nifty gnome helpers. Everyone except Gromit, who was rushing around, trying to keep watch over them. The Norbot army was relentless, mowing down everything in its way.

Wallace watched his gnomes on screen with pride. 'The Norbot army are a triumph, Gromit!' he shouted into the intercom. 'We'll soon have those bills paid off!'

Gromit didn't hear him. Gnome-tracking was hard work. Especially when the Norbot

army seemed to be targeting him, throwing tiles on his paws and rolling turf over him. They clearly didn't like dogs – or was it just Gromit? As he peered over a fence to try to see what they were up to, a gnome yanked the nails out of a fence plank. Gromit crashed forward on to a waiting trampoline and bounced ***BOING!*** into a wheelbarrow that the Norbot army had set up.

The wheelbarrow whizzed along and suddenly stopped, throwing Gromit into a garden shed. With a ***BANG!*** a gnome slammed the door shut and stuck a plant pot in front of it. It was a trap! The Norbot army wasn't stupid. In fact, it was extremely 'Smart' – and the gnomes knew that Gromit didn't trust them.

Gromit was trapped. He pressed his face against the shed window and watched in dismay as the original Norbot and his army marched through the garden towards the van.

As Gromit banged helplessly on the window, the original Norbot turned round and saluted Gromit with an evil grin. He'd tricked him!

The Norbot army marched into the van and drove off. The van seemed to be very heavy and chugged its way along at a slow and ponderous pace. It was clearly weighed down with more than just gnomes – but what else could be inside?

The original Norbot headed directly to 62 West Wallaby Street and reversed into Wallace's garage. Quick as a flash, the gnomes jumped out and slammed the garage door shut.

Nobody could see what was in the van. And that's exactly what the Norbot army wanted.

Chapter Ten

THINGS GO MISSING

Mr and Mrs Lovejoy were enjoying a lovely birthday celebration in their garden. Their lawn had just been trimmed by the Norbot army and they were very pleased with the results.

'Happy Birthday, Mavis,' said Mr Lovejoy, carrying a celebration cake to the garden table.

Mavis Lovejoy was delighted. 'Oh, smashing,' she said, eagerly awaiting her iced sponge.

CRASH! As Mr Lovejoy put the plate onto the table, it dropped straight to the ground and smashed into pieces. Jammy sponge and icing splattered all over the lawn. The glass tabletop had completely disappeared!

'Oh!' said a shocked Mavis. 'What happened to my table?'

At a nearby house, Mr Dibber opened his shed door to find it completely bare.

'Where's me tools?' he exclaimed, looking in all the corners.

Over the road, Mrs Gazebo was in an even worse state.

'Where's me SHED?' she gasped in dismay. Her entire garden shed had disappeared, leaving just the floor and the door standing on its own.

All over town, angry customers were discovering that they had been robbed. Lawnmowers, spades, deckchairs, gazebos . . . you name it – they were gone.

At the police station, a frantic PC Mukherjee was trying to cope with all the complaints.

'Another burglary? What's the address?' she gabbled, picking up the phone. 'Your weathervane's missing?'

RING RING! The phone calls kept on coming.

'Someone's pinched your big butt?' said a surprised Mukherjee. 'Oh, WATER butt!'

She pressed another pin to a large wall map of the village, which showed the locations of all the robberies.

An irritated Chief Inspector Mackintosh emerged to see what all the commotion was about. He grabbed the phone before Mukherjee could answer the next call and put on his best answerphone voice.

'Hello. You have reached the Old Bill. We're experiencing a high volume of calls at the moment, so please leave your crime after the beep. ***BEEP!***' he uttered, slamming the phone down.

'PC Mukherjee – what is going on here?' he demanded.

'Oh, Chief,' said Mukherjee, excitedly. 'It's a spate of burglaries. Like, a proper crime wave.'

'I can't be dealing with a crime wave!' cried the inspector. 'I've got enough on my hands as it is!' He held up two ties to show Mukherjee. 'Which one do you think – blue or black for the Grand Opening?'

Mukherjee was rather taken aback. 'Er – blue?' she said.

'Yes, I see what you're saying,' said the inspector, holding up the tie and admiring himself in the mirror. 'The blue matches the diamond.'

'Any road – about these robberies,' said Mukherjee, trying to bring the subject back to crime. 'I've been building this crime wall.' She pointed to her map. 'Trying to find common themes and such.'

The inspector looked at the photos of the victims, with their stolen goods displayed. 'Never mind "crime walls", Mukherjee!' he said. 'What's your copper's gut telling you?' He patted his belly, wisely.

'Well,' said PC Mukherjee. 'All the clues seem to point to *this* man.' She tapped a photograph of Wallace. 'A local inventor.'

'Wallace?' exclaimed the inspector. 'The upstanding citizen who helped put Feathers behind bars?' He thought about it for a moment. 'Yeah, why not? Catching one super villain doesn't make you a saint, does it?'

'Should we say he's a suspect, then?' asked PC Mukherjee.

'Just bring him in and book him,' said the inspector, sharply. 'Job done.'

Mukherjee looked shocked.

'The sooner he's banged to rights, the sooner I can get back to writing my speech,' continued the inspector.

'But – don't we need evidence?' said Mukherjee. The inspector laughed and rolled his eyes.

'All these fancy ideas you get from training college!' he sighed. He put on his police hat.

'Right,' he said. 'Come on, then!'

CHAPTER ELEVEN

GNOMES AT WORK

Still trapped in the garden shed, Gromit was now using the blade of an old tin opener to carefully saw through the wall. ***THUNK!***

A perfectly Gromit-shaped piece of corrugated iron crashed down onto the ground and the determined dog stepped through, ready for action. Enough of this gnome-sense! It was time to sort the Norbot army out.

At home, Wallace was relaxing on the sofa, unaware that a gnomish nightmare had been unleashed upon the neighbourhood.

'News just in,' came Anton Deck's voice from the TV. 'We're getting reports of a crime wave affecting gardens across the region! Onya Doorstep has more.'

The original Norbot heard the headline and rushed into the room. He didn't want Wallace hearing about this. Stepping smartly in front of the TV, he switched channels. **CLICK!** An old science-fiction movie came on.

'Aaah!' screamed the actress, in terror. 'The

robots are taking over the world! They'll destroy us all!' Norbot thought it best to turn the TV off altogether.

Wallace looked up from his magazine.

'That's a bit hasty, Norbot!' he said. 'I might have been watching that!'

'Time to relax, Mr Wallace,' said Norbot.

Another gnome came in, dragging a harp. **WHOOSH!** He lit the fire with a concealed flamethrower, then began playing sweet lullabies on his instrument. More gnomes entered with footrests and a cosy blanket for Wallace.

'Massage, Mr Wallace?' said a gnome, placing a small step ladder behind Wallace. He climbed it and began massaging his head and ears.

'Ooh, that's lovely,' said Wallace, enjoying the ear-rub. 'You *are* spoiling me!'

Another gnome came in with a tray of steaming mugs.

'Snoozy Choc?' asked the original Norbot.

'Don't mind if I do,' said a happy Wallace, slurping the hot chocolate. 'Mmmm!'

'Drink up, Mr Wallace!' said another gnome, tipping the Snoozy Choc into Wallace's mouth.

'Oh, steady on,' muttered a dozy Wallace. He hiccupped quietly, then closed his eyes and began to snore. The Snoozy Choc had done its job. The original Norbot grinned and left, closing the door.

A scooter screeched to a halt outside, but Wallace heard nothing.

It was Gromit. He leapt off and headed to the garage to find the van. The garage was empty. Gromit raised an eyebrow and went into the house.

Hearing the sound of snoring, he peered round the door of the sitting room to see Wallace, fast asleep, surrounded by empty mugs. Gromit's ears twitched. As well as the snoring there was another sound – the harsh noise of hammering, grinding and scraping. It was coming from the basement.

WELCOME TO 62 WEST WALLABY STREET!

62 West Wallaby Street is the home of Wallace and Gromit. The ever-expanding basement is where Wallace's cracking contraptions come to life. Over the years, the house has contained a windmill-powered bakery, a factory for knitted goods and even a launchpad for a rocket!

Whatever the adventure, however, Wallace and Gromit can often be found with their feet up in the living room, sipping on a hot cuppa with a plate of their favourite cheese and crackers.

WALLACE

Wallace is a genius inventor from the north of England. The only thing he loves more than inventing and cheese is his best friend and loyal pooch, Gromit.

Wallace's contraptions tend to be unnecessarily complicated, but they improve everyday objects in ways you could never imagine. His 'can do' attitude and endlessly positive nature means he doesn't always consider the consequences of his inventions, which sometimes gets him into trouble!

All the same, Wallace hasn't got a bad bone in his body. His affection for his old friend, Gromit, is at the heart of everything he does.

GROMIT

Gromit is the loyal, long-suffering, silent sidekick of his owner and best friend, Wallace. He prefers the quiet life: gardening, reading, the arts, drinking tea and knitting.

But, despite Gromit's quiet exterior, he is razor sharp, fast-thinking, ingenious and fearless in the face of danger. When Wallace finds himself in trouble (as he often does), Gromit always comes to the rescue!

He will go to the ends of the earth to save his beloved friend. (And still be home in time to put the kettle on.)

GOOD NORBOT

Norbot is one of Wallace's greatest inventions – a smart gnome who has been pre-programmed to do any kind of gardening task or home improvement.

Norbot is a quick learner, and no job is too small or too much trouble. His core protocol is to always do good and help others.

He is endlessly polite, cheerful and happy to help. He does everything he's told and works tirelessly without the need for any tea breaks – just plug him in at night and he's raring to go again the next morning.

EVIL NORBOT

When **Norbot** is 'hacked' by dark forces, his core protocol is changed and he becomes a very different gnome . . .

- Curt responses
- Always watching you
- Evil intentions

While he remains outwardly polite and attentive, Evil Norbot is actually busy building and organizing an army of smart gnomes that wreak havoc around town! Unless Gromit can stop Evil Norbot, it looks like Wallace is in danger of being outsmarted by his own smart gnome!

OFFICERS OF THE LAW

CHIEF INSPECTOR MACKINTOSH

Chief Inspector Mac is an experienced copper with an impressive (albeit slightly exaggerated) success record. Though he sometimes grasps the wrong end of the stick, he always makes sure justice is served in the end.

PC MUKHERJEE

PC Mukherjee is fresh out of training and desperate to prove herself as a new copper. She's bright, enthusiastic, hard-working and very thorough in her investigations.

FEATHERS MCGRAW

A true super-villain and master of disguise (thanks to his skills with a red rubber glove), the inscrutable **Feathers McGraw** always has an evil scheme on the go. He is calculating, conniving and incredibly clever. If he sets his mind on something, he stops at nothing to get it.

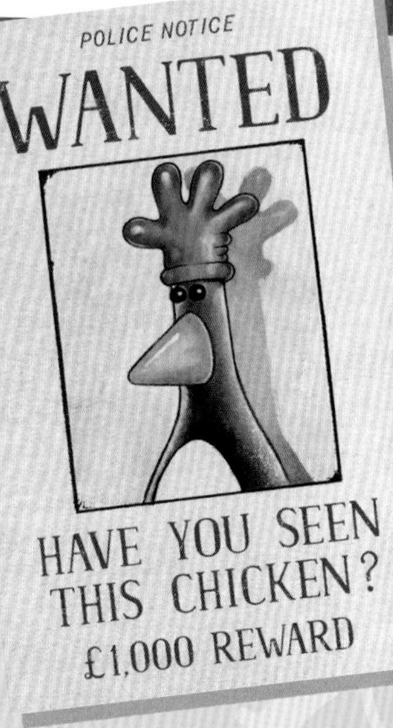

But, much like an iceberg, most of what's going on with Feathers lies well hidden beneath the surface, making him a difficult foe. Underestimate him at your peril.

THE ZOO

Years ago, when **Feathers McGraw** was thwarted in his efforts to steal the Blue Diamond, he was taken to the local zoo, which was modified to act as the villain's lock-up. Feathers's cell led to the penguin enclosure, where he was to spend his sentence being watched by the public and picking up litter.

The police and zookeepers thought Feathers's enclosure would be secure enough to stop any new evil plans. But this scheming and vengeful penguin has always got a trick up his sleeve. (Or in his rubber glove . . .)

Gromit rushed to the basement door and peered through the keyhole. The Norbot army was in there, hard at work. But what were they doing? Gromit needed a closer look. He ran outside and opened up the old coal hatch, then abseiled down on a rope. Once inside, he hid in the shadows. Gromit's eyes widened as he took in the busy industrial scene that was happening before him.

Gnomes were scurrying about everywhere. There were Norbots wielding clipboards, Norbots pushing trolleys and Norbots banging hammers. Other Norbots were wearing safety goggles and using welding tools. Sparks flew as Norbots melted down drainpipes, signs, weathervanes and all the other stolen items from the village, hammering them into new pieces. The finished pieces were being hoisted over to a large tarpaulin surrounded by scaffolding. There was something big and oval-shaped underneath it. Gromit narrowed his eyes and worked out what was happening. The Norbot army had stolen all the villagers' things – and they were making them into something.

Gromit had to find out what was under that tarpaulin.

Chapter Twelve

A SHOCK FOR GROMIT

Keeping well out of sight, Gromit dodged through the crowds of busy gnomes towards the tarpaulin. He finally reached it and carefully began to lift a corner. Just as he was about to see underneath, there was a loud ***SQUEAK!*** Gromit looked down in horror. He had trodden on a squeaky plastic duck!

The whole basement fell silent. The Norbot army slowly turned to look at Gromit. All he could do was try to distract them. With a casual

shrug, he picked up the duck and offered it to the gnomes. He squeaked it. Then he turned and fled up the steps as fast as his paws would take him!

Gromit rushed into the sitting room. He had to wake Wallace up and tell him what was happening! ***SPLASH!*** He threw a jug of freezing water over his snoozing master's head, but the dozy inventor simply carried on snoring. Gromit stopped to think, then rushed off again. Moments later, he returned carrying the **PAT-O-MATIC** machine.

Gromit twiddled the settings from **V. GOOD DOG** to **TOP DOG** and placed the device next to his master's head. ***SLAP! SLAP! SLAP!*** Wallace's cheeks got a vigorous pasting. He spluttered and finally opened his eyes.

'Gromit!' he said, irritably. 'What on earth . . .?' Then he saw Gromit pointing at the hallway in a panic.

'What? Is something wrong?' said Wallace. 'Is it the Norbot army?' Gromit nodded, fiercely. He grabbed Wallace's arm and led him down to the basement.

'This had better be important, lad,' grumbled Wallace. 'I don't know what's got into you lately.' Gromit threw open the basement door to show him everything that was going on. But he didn't get the reaction he expected. Wallace's face lit up.

'Well, I'll go to the top of my stairs!' he said, with a smile. 'That's absolutely – **SPOTLESS!**'

A confused Gromit did a double take as he peered into the basement. It *was* spotless! Moments ago, the whole place had been mayhem, a factory floor of heat and noise. But now it had all gone.

The mystery tarpaulin, the hammers, welding tools and all the stolen items had vanished into thin air. The gnomes were cleaning up, looking sweet and innocent. Gromit's mouth dropped open.

'Oh, you are good gnomes, doing all these chores at this time of night,' said Wallace. He glared at Gromit. 'I don't know why you were so keen to show me, you daft pooch. Couldn't it have waited till morning?' But Gromit was still staring at the basement, wondering how the gnomes had transformed it so quickly.

The original Norbot sidled up and slipped his arm through Gromit's, as if he were his best friend. Gromit shook him off and narrowed his eyes at the nasty gnome.

'You daft pooch!' said Wallace. He yawned and stretched. 'Well, I've got a nap to finish before I turn in for the night.' Wallace headed back upstairs, leaving Gromit behind. The gnomes stared at him in sinister silence.

The quiet was interrupted by a loud **BANG! BANG!** on the front door.

'Did you order a pizza, lad?' called Wallace from the stairs. He headed for the hall while the knocking continued.

'All right, all right, hold your horses!' he said. As he opened the door, he cried out in alarm. A fierce-looking police constable was charging towards him with a battering ram!

'POLICE!' shouted PC Mukherjee, falling through the open door and landing in a heap on the floor. 'Oops – sorry!' she added, sitting up.

Chief Inspector Mackintosh was right behind her. 'Give me strength!' he said, rolling his eyes. 'Right – let's get this over with.'

Wallace looked shocked. 'Get *what* over with?' he said. The inspector flashed a piece of paper at Wallace and pushed past.

'We have a warrant to search your premises. Mukherjee, read him his rights.'

'Yes, sir,' said PC Mukherjee, now recovered from her fall. She cleared her throat. 'Anything you say may be taken down and used as evidence against you.'

'But I haven't done anything!' cried Wallace.

PC Mukherjee looked him in the eye. 'We believe you to be guilty of "theft-by-gnome"!'

Gromit clapped a paw to his forehead. This was just what he'd been afraid of.

Wallace was stunned. 'I'm guilty of "theft-by-gnome"?' he repeated.

'Ha! There you go. He admits it,' said the inspector, triumphantly. 'Write that down.'

Wallace wasn't having any of it. 'This is ridiculous,' he protested. 'My Norbots aren't thieves. They're down in my workshop right now, doing a bit of spring cleaning.'

'That's our evidence, Chief!' Mukherjee cried.

'All right. Check them out, then,' said the inspector. But PC Mukherjee was already gone. She burst into the basement, brandishing her torch like a weapon, and shone it around. The inspector followed her and clicked on the light.

The basement was empty.

'Well,' said a confused Wallace, 'the Norbots were here a moment ago. They must have popped out to finish a job.'

The inspector glared at Wallace. 'I have not got time for your games, sunshine,' he said, storming off.

'Where are you going, Chief?' asked PC Mukherjee.

'I'm off to get my 'tache trimmed,' the inspector announced. 'For the big day!'

He turned to his PC 'If you need evidence, Mukherjee – find some! I want this case wrapped up, pronto.' With that, he left, slamming the door.

'Understood, sir,' said Mukherjee, looking around. 'Right, evidence.' Off she went to search the house.

Wallace and Gromit looked at each other. What was she looking for? And what on earth was 'theft by gnome'?

Meanwhile, PC Mukherjee was discovering plenty of suspicious-looking gadgets.

'Calling for back-up,' she said into her police radio. 'We'll need a van. A big one!'

CHAPTER THIRTEEN

NO GADGETS, NO NORBOTS

The next morning – ***BRRIINNGG!*** – off went Gromit's alarm clock. Wallace's voice came over the intercom. 'Gromit, get me up, lad! There's a good pooch!' But Gromit's bed was empty. He was down in the basement, surveying the mess following yesterday's police raid. Yellow crime-scene tape was plastered everywhere and all of Wallace's gadgets and inventions had been taken to the police station, leaving loose wires and empty spaces.

Gromit looked around, wondering where the Norbot army could have hidden all their stolen goods. And where was the secret thing they were building? Discovering a stethoscope, Gromit checked the walls to see if there were any empty spaces behind them. But he couldn't find anything.

In his bed, Wallace stretched, wondering why Gromit hadn't operated the **GET-U-UP DELUXE**. Suddenly he remembered the events of the day before. 'Wait a mo',' he said, scratching his head. 'The police have taken away all my inventions, for forensic examination or something. Outrageous!'

He stepped out of bed – and with a ***CRASH!*** fell straight into a hole in the floor where the chute used to be. In the basement, Gromit jumped in shock as the noisy vibrations came down the stethoscope.

'Argh!' Wallace shouted, pulling himself out

of the hole. Dusting himself down, he looked around for his clothes. 'Who needs technology anyway?' he said as he started to get dressed. 'Not me!'

Wallace hadn't dressed himself for years without the help of his inventions.

He tried to put his socks on – but he soon lost his balance and began hopping around the room. With only one sock on, he hopped into a mop bucket. It whizzed uncontrollably onto the landing, and catapulted Wallace directly into the bath with a loud ***SPLASH!***

'Argh, that's nippy!' shouted Wallace from the freezing water. His warming bubble-bath device had been taken away to the police station. But worse was to come. The bath began whizzing along its tracks and came to a halt, tossing Wallace through a hole in the side wall of the house, where a chute had once been. Wallace was hurled through the air like a cannon ball. He landed in a flower bed with a loud ***THUD!***

'Ooh, me begonias!' he winced. 'I think I need a cup of tea, lad!'

Gromit was still trying to find answers in the basement, but failing. He angrily kicked an old paint can, which knocked against a cupboard. Hearing Wallace's cries, Gromit stomped up the basement steps to deal with his master. As he slammed the basement door, the cupboard wobbled and a jam jar of water sitting on top of it toppled over. The jar smashed and water spilt everywhere. Slowly, the water ran across the floor – and disappeared into the gaps. So there *was* a hidden space – underground!

Managing to haul himself up, Wallace limped, dazed and half dressed, into the house. Gromit was there, reaching for the dusty old teapot on the shelf. Wallace's tea-making gadget

had been taken away and they would have to have a brew the old way.

Wallace stared at the teapot and pressed the knob on the lid. 'I haven't used one of these for so long I've forgotten how they work,' he said, scratching his head. He waited expectantly. Nothing happened.

'It's broken,' said a cross Wallace, pushing

the teapot off the table. Gromit dived and caught it, just in time, but Wallace didn't even notice. He was too busy thinking about how unfairly the police had treated him.

'There's clearly been a mistake. My Norbots are innocent!' he cried, looking at Gromit. 'You believe me, don't you, lad?' Gromit looked down at his feet, miserably. He wanted to believe Wallace, but he didn't. He didn't trust *any* of the Norbot army.

'Don't you, lad?' repeated Wallace. Gromit shook his head in sorrow.

Wallace's face crumpled. 'Oh. Well,' he said. Then his tone changed. 'You've never trusted my Norbot, have you?' he said, waving his finger at Gromit. 'And I made him just for you! Mark my words – the police will be back soon to apologize.'

A loud ***KNOCK KNOCK!*** was heard at the door.

'What did I tell you?' said Wallace, opening it. 'There they are now. Everything will be right as rain before you can say . . .'

'NASTY CROOKED THIEVING LITTLE TOERAG!' came a loud shout. In front of him was a huge crowd of loud, angry people, holding banners. Yells of 'Where's our stuff?' and 'I want me barbecue back!' could be heard. Wallace stepped back in shock, as Onya Doorstep appeared with her news crew.

'I'm live on TV outside the West Wallaby Street home of the evil inventor, Mr Wallace!' she announced into her microphone.

'E-evil?' stuttered Wallace. 'Don't you mean "smart-thinking"?'

'You think it's **SMART** to teach gnomes to **STEAL**?' cried Onya, thrusting her microphone into Wallace's face.

'If only my gnomes were here, maybe I could clear my name!' said a panicked Wallace.

'Well, where *are* the gnomes?' questioned Onya.

'I don't know!' said Wallace, in desperation.

The angry crowd got even angrier. They began to chant. **'WHERE ARE THE GNOMES? WHERE ARE THE GNOMES?'** Things were not looking good for poor Wallace. From inside his cell, Feathers McGraw listened to the news as it boomed out from the zookeepers' TV. As the shouts and jeers of the crowd got louder, the penguin's black beady eyes gleamed with satisfaction.

Everything was going exactly to plan.

Chapter Fourteen

GROMIT ON THE MOVE

Wallace stumbled back inside the hall and closed the front door on the shouting hordes.

'How am I supposed to find my gnomes when the police have taken my Gnome Tracker?' he asked Gromit, in desperation. Gromit thought for a moment. Then he had an idea.

Rushing into the garage, he jumped into the van and switched on the engine. There was silence. Gromit tried again, but nothing happened. He hopped out and looked at the vehicle. There was no engine. There were no wheels! The Norbot army had taken them, leaving Wallace and Gromit stranded!

But wait! Gromit pulled a dustsheet off to reveal – their trusty motorbike and sidecar!

VROOM! In minutes, Gromit was zooming to the police station.

The only way to prove that Wallace was innocent was to find those gnomes!

At the station, Chief Inspector Mackintosh was shouting at PC Mukherjee. The station was cluttered with Wallace's gadgets and the inspector wasn't happy.

'Never mind Scotland Yard!' cried the inspector. 'It looks more like a scrapyard in here!'

'It's Wallace's stuff, Chief,' said PC Mukherjee. 'You told me to find some evidence.'

'I didn't mean take the whole flipping house!' said the inspector. 'I mean – what's this in aid of?' He pressed a red button on Wallace's **PAT-O-MATIC**.

SLAP! SLAP! SLAP! The automatic hand gave the inspector a very sound patting. 'Ow! Aah! Geroff!' yelled the inspector, dropping the device. 'That gizmo just assaulted a police officer!' he shouted. 'Add that to the list of charges, Mukherjee!'

Mukherjee sighed and rubbed her tired eyes. She'd spent the whole night inspecting Wallace's inventions.

'That's just it, Chief,' she said. 'I've been through everything. There's nothing here to pin Wallace to the burglaries. I'm getting the feeling that he's not our man!

The inspector wasn't impressed. 'They're *his* gnomes, aren't they?' he said. 'Wallace is a wrong un! End of story.'

Arriving at the police station, Gromit jumped off the motorbike and entered the reception area, where he could see the inspector and PC Mukherjee having a loud discussion. Gromit took his chance and dropped down on

the floor, completely out of sight. He crawled underneath the reception counter and silently made his way across the floor to where Wallace's gadgets were.

'Now, if you don't mind, we'll deal with this later,' said the inspector, crossly. 'We've got much more important things to attend to up at the museum.'

'But, sir . . . ' said PC Mukherjee.

The inspector ignored her and carried on. 'It's my big day, Mukherjee,' he said, proudly. 'The culmination of forty years of service. Everyone who's anyone is coming to see the Blue Diamond go back on display. **NOTHING** can go wrong.'

As he spoke, Wallace's Gnome Tracker Radar Dish began slowly and silently moving across the room. It glided towards the reception area, and out of the building. Neither the inspector nor PC Mukherjee noticed a thing.

'We have to stay focused,' he said. 'Watch like hawks! Miss **NOTHING!**'

'Yes, sir!' said PC Mukherjee.

Outside the station, Gromit attached the Gnome Tracker Radar Dish and screen to the motorbike and switched them on. The dish began to rotate. ***BLEEP! BLEEP! BLEEP!*** The radar was on full alert. It was a foggy night, but Gromit very much hoped that no gnome would be left unturned.

Gromit rode off, keeping a careful eye on the screen. Suddenly ***BLEEEEEEEP!*** The volume increased and lots of little gnome icons appeared on the screen. Gnome alert!

Gromit tried his best to see through the foggy swirls, but it wasn't easy. Up ahead, he spotted a row of pointy heads. Gromit's ears twitched in anticipation, but as he got closer they flopped down in disappointment. It was a pile of traffic cones on the back of a lorry. But now the lorry was coming towards him fast and its headlights shone in Gromit's eyes. ***TOOOOT!*** Its horn sounded as Gromit swerved to avoid a collision. He plummeted down a steep bank and came to a standstill at the bottom. He was next to a large wall.

BLEEP! BLEEP! The gnome warning was getting louder. Gromit gulped and looked around, straining to see through the fog. He couldn't see any gnomes. He nervously grabbed a fishing net from the sidecar to defend himself.

On screen, the gnome icons were coming straight towards him. ***BLEEP! BLEEP!*** Now they were on him! What was going on? Gromit stared at the screen in confusion. Suddenly, he realized what was happening. He looked down to see a drain with a metal grille over the top, lights moving underneath it. The tracker was picking up the gnomes from below.

The gnomes were travelling **UNDERGROUND!**

Looking up, Gromit saw a high wall, covered in barbed wire, and a sign saying **ZOO**.

The Norbot army was going to the zoo. But why?

Gromit didn't know, but he was going to climb that wall. Because if the gnomes were going to the zoo so was Gromit!

Chapter Fifteen

WHAT A TO-DO IN THE ZOO!

But how would Gromit get past that wall?

He looked around and spotted a large tree with a branch that stuck out over the wall. Gromit grabbed his retractable dog lead and threw it like a lasso round the branch. He pushed the button on the handle. **ZOOOM!** The lead retracted, pulling Gromit up the tree. Crawling along the branch, Gromit peered at the view through his binoculars.

He soon spotted the penguin enclosure,

where a high-backed black swivel chair stood. It spun round.

Gromit almost dropped his binoculars as he realized that sitting in the chair was none other than **FEATHERS MCGRAW!**

He was stroking a white baby seal like a pet – and he looked incredibly evil. Gromit gulped. Was this Feathers's high-security prison?

POP! A plastic duck popped out of the penguin pool. It was attached to a long periscope made from an old drainpipe. The periscope was attached to something else. Something big! With a **WHOOSH!** a mini submarine suddenly rose up from the water, right in front of Gromit's eyes!

So this was what the gnomes had been building! A submarine made from all the pilfered parts: bathtubs, drainpipes, glass tabletops and more.

CLANG! The submarine hatch shot open and out jumped the army of gnomes. They lined up smartly and saluted their master – Feathers

McGraw. Feathers stood up and walked the line to inspect them, as if they were members of his own Gnome navy. The penguin moved to step on board the submarine, but, before he did, he pulled on his red-glove disguise. Then he turned and looked directly at Gromit, his beady eyes as cold as ice.

Gromit gulped. Feathers *knew* that Gromit was watching him!

Before he could work out his next move, Gromit heard a horrible sound. ***URRRR EEEE, URRRR EEEE!*** He turned to see the original Norbot cutting through his branch with a saw. In the distance, Feathers McGraw gave Gromit a last salute as if to say goodbye. The branch snapped and both Gromit and Norbot plummeted to the ground.

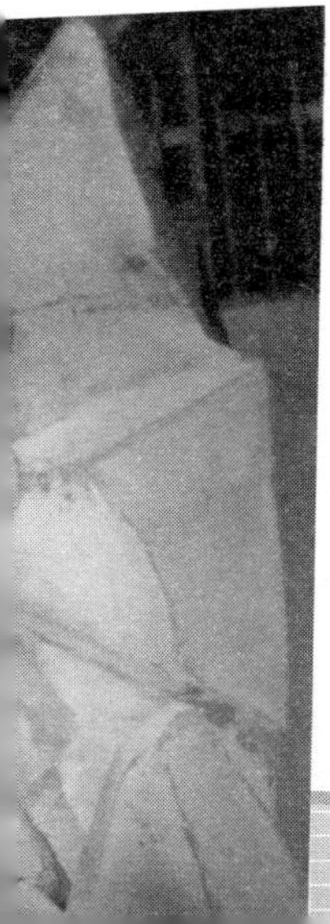

CRASH! As Gromit fell, he grabbed hold of a **DO NOT FEED** sign that fell beside him. Norbot then landed with a **CLICK!** that jolted his system.

'Reset mode activated,' said Norbot.

A dazed Gromit stood up to see the submarine descending into the water of the penguin pool. It disappeared with a bubbling sound. Then he heard a low roar – and a dark lion-shaped shadow loomed over him. Gromit turned to see the teeth and mane of a huge and very angry lion. He and Norbot had fallen into the **BIG-CAT** enclosure!

The lion roared and leapt at Gromit. He was hungry! Gromit grabbed the **DO NOT FEED** sign and rammed it into the lion's mouth. Before the surprised creature could crunch it up, Gromit was gone. He'd seen his dog lead lying on the ground and thrown it over the wall, pulling himself to safety.

Norbot suddenly sat up. 'Restored to inventor settings!' he said, cheerily. His system had reset – and now it was back to **GOOD!** The lion watched warily as Norbot, no longer evil, got to his feet. Gromit watched in horror from high up.

'Hi,' said Norbot, happily. 'I'm your Nifty Odd-jobbing Robot. Call me Norbot.' In seconds, Norbot had produced a pair of scissors. 'Initiating pruning process!' he said, and began trimming the shocked lion's mane.

'Neat and tidy!' said Norbot, finishing off.

ROARRR! The lion didn't like his new square hair. He snarled and raised his claws to attack the bearded barber. But, before the lion could pounce, a heroic Gromit reached out and pulled Norbot out of harm's way. The Smart Gnome was saved!

A hurried Gromit led Norbot back to the motorbike. He checked the Gnome Tracker again. ***BLEEP! BLEEP!*** Feathers and his Norbot army were heading for the town museum via an underground sewer. The Blue Diamond!

There was no time to lose. Gromit put Norbot in the sidecar and jumped on the bike. Off they zoomed to the museum.

'No job is too small!' said Norbot, giving the Gnome Tracker screen a good clean as they whizzed down the road.

Chapter Sixteen

MUSEUM MAYHEM

The museum was buzzing with hordes of guests and reporters, all waiting for a glimpse of the famous Blue Diamond. Soon the gleaming gem would be revealed to the excited crowds before going on display to the public.

The man to reveal the diamond was none other than Chief Inspector Mackintosh. Dressed in his best suit and tie, he stood proudly in front of an empty glass case. In front of him was a small bag containing the precious diamond.

The stone had been locked up in the high-security museum vault ever since Feathers McGraw had been captured – and this was the first time that it had been taken out.

The ceremony began. 'It's been my great pride over the years to serve this community,' announced the inspector. 'Knowing there's nothing more reassuring than the sight of an uninformed officer . . .'

There was an awkward silence and PC Mukherjee coughed.

'Sorry!' said the inspector. 'UNIFORMED police officer! Can't read my own writing. Anyway, now I have one final happy duty to perform.'

VROOM! Outside the building, Gromit screeched up on the motorbike, with Norbot wobbling in the sidecar. The dynamic dog took a deep breath and rode the bike, **BUMPITY BUMP**, all the way up the museum steps, where he leapt off the bike and ran to the entrance. The doors were locked. A sign said **MUSEUM CLOSED FOR PRIVATE EVENT**. Gromit rushed to a window, but it was barred. He narrowed his eyes and tried to peer inside.

He could see the chief inspector with the bag in front of him. Gromit watched intently as the big reveal of the Blue Diamond took place.

'Here we are, ladies and gentlemen,' announced the inspector, opening the bag. 'Safely on display for future generations – the **BLUE DIAMOND!**' He tipped the contents gently into his hand and held it out to the side for public viewing. Cameras flashed and people gasped.

'It's not as shiny in real life, is it?' remarked the mayor.

'You what?' said the inspector, turning to see that he was holding – a mouldy turnip!

'That's a flipping turnip!' he cried, dropping it in horror.

Everyone started talking, excitedly. PC Mukherjee racked her brains.

'You did check *inside*

the bag, Chief, before you put it in the vault all that time ago?' she asked.

The inspector looked unsure. 'Ummm,' he said, trying vainly to remember. Suddenly his face fell. He remembered now. He had put the bag safely into the vault and waited as the guards locked it up – but, as he was eager to get to the pub, he hadn't checked inside it.

Mukherjee couldn't believe it. 'So – if you've been guarding a turnip all these years,' she cried, 'where's the Blue Diamond?'

Outside the window, Gromit's eyes widened in amazement. How had a turnip got into the diamond bag?

He had no idea – but he did know that Feathers McGraw had something to do with it. Gromit rushed to the motorbike and checked the Gnome Tracker. ***BLEEP! BLEEP!*** Feathers and the gnomes were in the submarine – and the submarine was on the move. But where?

Chapter Seventeen

TEAPOT TURMOIL

Back at West Wallaby Street, Wallace was alone, playing a sad tune on his piano.

'Gnomes have gone, gadgets are gone, even me dog's gone,' he said to himself. He'd never felt more miserable.

All of a sudden, the piano began to wobble and loud vibrations shook the room.

'What on earth?' uttered Wallace, looking around in a panic. The shaking seemed to be coming from the basement. Wallace ran to the basement door and opened it, peering down the stairs. The floor was sliding open to reveal a giant square hole!

'I didn't know it could do that!' said Wallace, in astonishment. There were more vibrations and noises as a large object began to rise up through the floor. Wallace couldn't believe his eyes. It was a submarine! Coming up from *his* basement!

At that moment, Gromit arrived outside. He glanced at the rumbling house with a worried expression, his ears twitching at the loud noises. Grabbing his cricket bat, he rushed through the front door, ready to fend off attackers. He was relieved to hear the sound of a familiar voice.

'Come in, Gromit! Everything's fine!' It was Wallace. Gromit lowered his bat and entered the sitting room. There was Wallace – but he was tied up and gagged!

An evil Norbot popped up next to Wallace.

'Everything's fine – just come straight in,' said the gnome in Wallace's voice. The robot gnome was using smart technology to impersonate Gromit's master!

Gromit was horrified. He had walked into a trap, and there was no escape. More evil Norbots appeared and, before he knew it, he was tied up with a sack over his head. Poor Gromit couldn't see a thing.

Time passed and eventually the sack was pulled off. Gromit blinked and realised that he was tied up to Wallace. The pair were sitting back to back on Wallace's wheeled office chair, surrounded by gnomes.

'Sorry, I couldn't warn you, lad,' muttered Wallace, shaking off his gag. 'I got grabbed by the Norbots. Very unpleasant experience.'

Gromit wriggled around, trying his hardest to squeeze out of the ropes.

'Turns out they are bad, after all,' continued

Wallace. 'I just don't get it. Why would my own gnomes turn against me?'

There was a sudden commotion, and the gnomes cleared a space. Their leader stepped forward.

'A chicken?' stuttered Wallace. 'Behind all this?'

Gromit rolled his eyes. The 'chicken' whipped off the red glove from his head. It was none other than master of disguise, Feathers McGraw!

'Good grief!' cried Wallace, in amazement. 'It's YOU! Again! But you're supposed to be locked up!' Feathers ignored him and glanced around the room. He was clearly looking for something.

'Whatever it is you're up to, you won't get away with it,' said an angry Wallace. Feathers spotted the old teapot on the shelf. The Norbot army got a ladder and took it down for him.

'Fancy a cup of tea, do you?' said Wallace, indignantly. 'The cheek of it! Well, I wouldn't bother with that teapot. It doesn't work.'

SMASH! All of a sudden, Feathers dropped the teapot onto the floor.

'What?' said a confused Wallace. The penguin leaned over and rummaged around in the broken pieces. Something glittered among the mess. It was a large diamond! Feathers picked it up and turned it round, entranced by its sparkle.

Wallace and Gromit were astonished. 'Well, butter me crumpets!' cried Wallace. 'It can't be! The Blue Diamond!' He thought for a moment about how it could have got into his teapot. Then it came to him. 'That penguin must have switched it all those years ago!'

Feathers had, indeed, switched the diamond. While Wallace had been busy calling the police, Feathers had been left alone in the kitchen with the diamond bag. The wily Feathers had wiggled out of his ropes and taken out the sparkling stone. He grabbed the teapot and placed the diamond inside, returning the pot to its place. A turnip from the vegetable rack was

just the right size to replace it in the bag. The cunning penguin knew that one day he would return to get the diamond for himself.

By the time the police had arrived, Feathers was back in the chair, safely tied up again, with the bag on the table. No one suspected a thing.

In all that time, the Blue Diamond had been sitting in Wallace's teapot!

'So that's your plan!' cried Wallace, suddenly catching on. 'You get away scot-free with the diamond and everyone thinks *I'm* the evil inventor that stole it. Why, that's – **VENGEANCE MOST FOWL!**'

Feathers gave Wallace a triumphant look. This was indeed his vengeance.

Before they could protest, Wallace and Gromit were pushed into the understairs cupboard by the evil gnomes. Feathers slammed the cupboard door shut, leaving them in darkness.

He made straight for the van and got into the driver's seat. The Norbot army jumped in too. They picked up the engine-less van and carried it, running down the street. ***BRRRMMM! BRRRMMM!!!*** went the gnome-powered van!

Chapter Eighteen

A WANTED WALLACE

A red-faced chief inspector burst out of the museum, furious about the turnip incident. PC Mukherjee followed him as he marched down the street.

'This is a disaster!' he cried. 'I'm the laughing stock of the town!'

'Should we haul Feathers in, Chief?' said Mukherjee. 'He had the diamond last.'

The inspector suddenly stopped. 'No!' he said. 'No – he didn't!'

'What?' said Mukherjee. 'You mean . . .?'

'Exactly!' said the inspector. They were both thinking of the same man. A certain bald-headed inventor who lived at 62 West Wallaby Street!

'Come on,' said the inspector, heading for their police bicycles.

His face fell when he saw his bike. Some thief had nicked his saddle!

There was nothing for it. The inspector jumped on the back of PC Mukherjee's bike.

'I can't believe someone's nicked me saddle,' he complained as they rode off, wobbling down the street.

'I know, sir,' panted Mukherjee, pedalling madly. 'Sorry, but you took me off that case!'

'Still, we've got our culprit! said the inspector, clinging on for dear life. 'All this time, Wallace just wanted the diamond for himself!'

'You were right all along, Chief,' gasped

Mukherjee. The inspector was no lightweight. 'He *is* a wrong un!"

'If Wallace thinks he's got away with this – he's got another think coming!' said the inspector.

Tied up in the dark cupboard, Wallace and Gromit were trying hard to get free. They were not succeeding.

'This is all my fault, lad,' said Wallace, glumly. 'I only ever wanted to invent good things, things that help people. I never imagined they could be used for . . . wrongdoing.'

Gromit's eyes welled up. Wallace had never meant anyone any harm.

CLOMP! CLOMP! CLOMP! Footsteps were heard approaching the cupboard.

'Oh no,' cried Wallace. 'It's the law! I'm done for.' The cupboard door creaked open.

'Morning, Mr Wallace. Master Gromit,' said the original Norbot, peering in to see the tied-up pair.

'Norbot!' cried Wallace. 'Where have you been?'

'No job is too small,' said Norbot, putting a leaf blower away in the cupboard.

'He's back to his nifty odd-jobbing self!' said a relieved Wallace. 'We're saved!'

'Neat and tidy!' said Norbot, taking out the vacuum cleaner and ignoring him. He closed the door on Wallace and Gromit and began hoovering the stairs.

'Norbot, come back!' shouted Wallace, above the noise. 'Don't worry, lad,' he said to Gromit. 'He's voice-activated. **NORBOT!**

NORBOT!' he cried. But Norbot couldn't hear him above the noise of the vacuum cleaner.

Wallace sank down, a broken man. But Gromit didn't give up so easily. He'd just had an idea that might get them out of there. He began to bounce up and down on the office chair.

'Steady on!' said a surprised Wallace. 'What are you up to, lad?' The chair began to move. Gromit kept bouncing and the chair hopped towards the leaf blower.

'Hardly the time to start leaf blowing!' said Wallace. Gromit ignored him and focused on working one leg free. With his foot, he flicked the switch of the leaf blower to ON.

WHOOOOSHH! A jet of air blasted out, sending the chair rocketing out of the cupboard and into the hallway. **CRASH!** They collided with Norbot. The gnome was sent soaring into the air, landing in Wallace's lap just as Gromit yanked the chair lever to make it horizontal.

WHEEEEE! All three of them went shooting off towards the front door on their jet-powered wheely chair.

Chief Inspector Mackintosh and Mukherjee had just arrived outside.

'Someone's got a big surprise coming,' said the inspector, grimly, stepping towards the front door. There was a loud cry of **'GROMMMMMMITTTTT!'** as the door was blasted outwards by a whizzing office chair, transporting a man, a dog and a gnome.

PC Mukherjee jumped out of the way just in time.

'Chief – they're getting away!' she shouted as the chair blasted past them. 'Chief?' Mukherjee looked at the front door lying on the ground. **DING DONG!** went the bell. She opened it. Underneath it was the flattened inspector.

'Did we get 'em?' he said, woozily.

Chapter Nineteen

THE BIG CANAL CHASE

The chair finally came to a standstill. A dazed Wallace looked up the street and spotted Feathers in the driving seat of the van.

'There's Feathers!' he shouted. 'Let's get after the bounder.' He and Gromit began to push themselves along on the office chair, using the wheels to help them gain speed.

'More speed, Mr Wallace?' said Norbot, turning the leaf blower up to TURBO BLOW. The trio blasted off and drew level with the van.

Feathers was staring straight ahead, his eyes on the road, the diamond bag on the passenger seat. Wallace levered the chair up and shouted through the window. 'Hand over the diamond, you little tyke! Norbot – fetch!'

A wobbly Norbot managed to clamber through the van window and reach out for the diamond bag, but Feathers spotted him and swerved down an alley to get away. A bin had fallen over and banana skins covered the ground. The sprinting gnomes slid on the slippery skins and the van spun round uncontrollably , turning over and landing upside down with a **CRASH!**

But Feathers wasn't hurt. He leapt out of the van, closely followed by the gnomes.

Slipping through a gap in a fence, he ran onto a towpath alongside a canal. In front of him was a narrow boat with a sign saying **THE PERFECT GETAWAY!** Feathers needed to get away. He hopped onto the boat, followed by the gnomes.

Behind them, Wallace, Gromit and Norbot had also swerved into the alley at high speed.

'Norbot! Stop this thing!' yelled Wallace.

'Yes, Mr Wallace,' said Norbot. He grabbed the rope that was tied round Wallace and lassoed a loop over a post.

'Not like **THAAAAT!**' shouted Wallace as the rope unravelled, making the chair spin madly. It rose into the air like a helicopter, flying over the fence. ***CRASH!*** They went through the roof of a second canal boat.

'Emergency stop, complete!' said Norbot.

Gromit recovered and sprang up. In front of them, Feathers's boat was chugging away. Not on Gromit's watch! He hotwired the boat and it revved into action. It was all systems go! Maximum speed! The chase was on! They moved off at a snail's pace, following Feathers and the Norbot army down the canal. Feathers looked behind and saw his pursuers, but couldn't get his boat to go any faster. The two canal boats chugged along slowly and were passed by an elderly lady walking her dog down the towpath. It was a chase like no one had ever seen before – and the most exciting thing that had ever happened on the canal.

PC Mukherjee and the inspector arrived on the bicycle. Mukherjee braked sharply on the canal bridge. 'There they are, Chief,' she shouted, spotting the boats.

'Nice-looking narrow boat that – a bit like mine,' said the inspector, casting his eye over the craft. He did a double take at its name, *Dun Nickin*. 'Hang on a sec! That *is* mine! **STOP IN THE NAME OF THE LAW!**' he shouted through a megaphone.

Gromit didn't hear him. He was too busy trying to steady the boat while ducking the many plant-pot missiles being thrown by the Norbot army in front. He dived through the exploding pots to find Wallace in the galley below.

'It's no use, lad!' Wallace cried, seeing Gromit. If only there was some way of rebooting the gnomes!'

CRASH! Another missile hit the boat and it lurched to one side. A cupboard opened up, spilling welly boots everywhere. Wallace emerged from the pile with a welly on his head and saw Gromit looking at him. At that moment they both knew what had to happen.

'Another invention?' said Wallace, spotting a toolbox. 'Are you sure, lad?' Gromit nodded slowly. He had never been surer in his life. Wallace brightened up.

'Right, then!' he said. 'Technical assistance is on its way!' He grabbed the toolbox with a gleam in his eye.

Chapter Twenty

WAR OF THE WELLIES

On the towpath, the two policemen cycled furiously after the boats chugging along the canal.

'I can't believe Wallace nicked my boat,' raged the inspector. 'And *you* thought he was innocent, Mukherjee!'

PC Mukherjee's eyes widened as she spotted a small black figure at the helm of the leading boat. 'I think that's Feathers McGraw,' she said. Suddenly she realized what was happening.

'Chief! Wallace and Gromit are trying to stop Feathers McGraw!'

Feathers heard her shouts and looked around. How had she recognized him? He patted his head and realized that he had lost his rubber-glove chicken disguise. With no time to lose, Feathers grabbed some black clothes and a scarf hanging up nearby and placed them over his head to cover himself up.

'Don't be ridiculous, Feathers McGraw is banged up in the zoo,' said the inspector, seeing a black-veiled figure at the helm through his binoculars. 'That's just an innocent nun out for a pleasure cruise!'

Mukherjee ignored him and pedalled off along the canal path as fast as she could.

'Waaah!' cried the inspector, almost falling off the bike.

'I think Wallace may have been unfairly portrayed as a crazed inventor,' panted

Mukherjee, cycling at top speed. At that exact moment, Wallace rose up through the roof of the boat. He was wearing safety goggles and operating some kind of bizarre boot-firing machine. **'HA HA HA!'** he cackled in glee.

Mukherjee gulped. 'Well, unfairly to a . . . certain extent.'

'**REBOOT-O-MATIC** in position, Gromit!' shouted Wallace, hitting switches and beginning to pedal his machine.

'What's he done with me vintage boot collection?' cried the outraged inspector, realizing that the **REBOOT-O-MATIC** was built from all his possessions.

'Let's give those gnomes a good reboot up the backside!' shouted Wallace, pulling a trigger and pedalling madly. The **REBOOT-O-MATIC** fired. Wellies shot out – ***PEW! PEW! PEW!*** The inspector and Mukherjee ducked to avoid the flying boots as they whizzed past their ears, firing straight into the gnomes. ***BOOM!*** All of the Norbot army were booted into the canal.

'Bullseye!' shouted Wallace.

'Reset mode activated!' reported the original Norbot.

'It's working, lad!' cried Wallace. 'Give it some more welly, Gromit!'

'This has gone far enough!' shouted the enraged inspector from the towpath. He got out his police radio. 'Chief Inspector Mac. All units pursue and arrest Wallace!'

A wayward welly came whizzing towards them. Mukherjee ducked but the inspector got the full impact. ***CLONK!*** He was knocked to the ground.

Mukherjee took over. 'Sorry, Chief, I'm using me gut,' she said, grabbing her radio. 'Calling all units! Head to the border. Suspect is **NOT** Wallace but a small nun in charge of a canal boat!'

She pedalled off after the boats, while the inspector got to his feet. He was fuming.

'You're in big trouble, Mukherjee!' he shouted after her, waving his fist.

CHAPTER TWENTY-ONE

AQUEDUCT ANTICS

Bearded heads began to pop up from the canal. The Norbots were smiling, even though they'd been hit with flying wellies and knocked into freezing water.

'Hi!' they said to each other. 'I'm Norbot, your Nifty Odd-jobbing Robot. Pleased to meet you!'

Wallace's **REBOOT-O-MATIC** had worked! Blasting the gnomes with wellies had set off their reset switches, and now they were back to their original **GOOD** selves!

Gromit grabbed a net and began fishing the gnomes out of the canal while Wallace kept his eyes on Feathers. 'Now we've got him!' he said, confidently. Then, 'Eh? Where's he gone?' as the penguin disappeared from view.

VROOM! The roar of an engine made them both jump. **SMASH!** Feathers's canal boat crashed through the gate of a boat-repair yard. The pesky penguin had customised his boat with new motors – and now it was transformed into a speed-canal-boat!

As it whizzed past Wallace and Gromit's boat, Feathers waved at them in triumph. Gromit moved fast. He threw a rope and lassoed a peg on the back of the speedboat.

'Well done, lad!' shouted Wallace. 'We've got **HIIIIMMM!**'

Their boat was suddenly dragged forward at high speed and Wallace tumbled off backwards with a **SPLASH!** Quick-thinking Gromit threw him a life ring.

'Don't let him get **AWAAAY!**' cried Wallace, rising into the air. Two old planks flew by and got caught under his feet. He was pulled into a standing position as he glided along the surface of the water. Wallace was waterskiing!

'Whoaa!' he cried, desperately trying to keep his balance.

Gromit grabbed a crank handle and began to wind in the rope, pulling their boat closer to Feathers's. Feathers saw what he was doing and rummaged through a handy picnic set. He discovered a cheese knife and began cutting through the rope. Gromit wound the rope even faster.

Behind them, Wallace swung wildly from one side of the canal to the other, as the boats whizzed down the waterway. He rose up in the air and veered over to the canal bank, heading directly into a small tent. **BOOF!** A shocked camper sitting on a chemical toilet was revealed as Wallace zoomed off, the tent wrapped round him.

'Oof, sorry!' shouted a muffled Wallace.

A low, dark tunnel was coming up. Gromit could see the diamond bag on the deck of Feathers's boat. But, just as they approached the tunnel entrance, Feathers finally sliced through the rope and it broke free. Gromit took his chance and made a leap. What a leap! He soared through the air and landed on Feathers's boat.

An airborne Wallace finally got free of the tent. With a toilet brush in his mouth, he crashed into a trailer full of root vegetables on the canal bank.

'Whoaa!' he cried as both he and the trailer sped off down the hill towards a clifftop.

'Huh?' said a bewildered farmer, looking around for his crop.

Meanwhile, Gromit had confronted Feathers on top of the boat. It was dog versus penguin. Feathers wielded an umbrella, fencing style, as they fought each other in the darkness, rolling around on the narrow roof. Feathers managed to pin the daring dog down, the umbrella across his neck. Things weren't looking good for Gromit.

At that moment, the boat emerged from the tunnel into the sunlight. It was now travelling across an incredibly high and dangerous-looking aqueduct!

Gromit and Feathers heard an 'AAAGHH!' and looked up to see Wallace flying off the clifftop towards them. *CRASH!* He smashed through the roof of the second canal boat, which was following behind. A shower of turnips and parsnips rained onto Feathers and Gromit.

Feathers tried to make his escape. He ran across the roof of the boat, just as Gromit leapt for him, pulling off his nun disguise. A shocked Feathers slapped Gromit across the face.

At that moment, PC Mukherjee and two police vans screeched to a halt at the far end of the aqueduct.

'I knew it was Feathers McGraw!' she cried, spotting the villainous penguin.

'Quick, close the gate!' Feathers saw the gates closing and slammed on the brakes. The boat spun round and Gromit was thrown up into the air. It came to a halt with each end hanging over the sides of the perilous aqueduct.

Everything went silent. There was an ominous **CREEEAAAAK!** as the boat see-sawed one way and the other in the wind. Gromit opened his eyes and found himself hanging by his paws from the bow, swinging in the breeze. He looked down at the huge drop, his eyes wide with fear At that moment, he realized that *he* was holding the diamond bag, not Feathers!

Feathers was at the opposite end of the boat, and he saw the precious bag at the same time. The reckless penguin began inching his way along the rocking boat towards Gromit. He wanted the Blue Diamond – and he'd risk anything to get it.

CREEAAAK! The boat began to rock dangerously, leaning heavily towards Gromit's side. Gromit gulped. If Feathers came any closer, the weight was going to bring the boat – and him – down!

Chapter Twenty-two

A GREAT ESCAPE

Feathers pointed at the diamond bag. He wanted Gromit to throw it to him. If he didn't, the penguin would move forward and make the entire boat – and its crew – fall from the aqueduct.

From the boat behind, Wallace could see Gromit's desperate position.

'Give him the diamond, lad!' he shouted. ' I can live without inventing.' Wallace's eyes filled with tears. 'But I can't live without my best pal!'

What was Gromit to do? He looked at the drop below and made up his mind. With seconds to spare, he tossed the bag to Feathers, who caught it with one flipper. Without blinking, the penguin walked backwards, grabbed his umbrella and jumped from the aqueduct, down, down, down, flicking the umbrella open as a parachute. He fell directly onto a steam train passing below. The lucky bird landed on an open wagon of squidgy Yorkshire puddings. Without Feathers's weight, the boat began tipping back to the other side. Gromit started to run up the leaning boat as it tipped upwards, sliding over the side of the aqueduct.

'NOOO!' shouted Wallace, lunging to save his pal. But it was too late. Gromit was plunging down to the ground.

'GRROOMMMIIIIT!' yelled Wallace as the pooch plummeted to his certain death.

CRASH! The boat hit the ground and smashed into pieces. Gromit, mid-air, closed his eyes, bracing himself for the same. But, just before impact, an arm shot out and grabbed him. A robot arm.

'Hi. I'm your Nifty Odd-jobbing Robot!' came a voice. 'Call me Norbot.' Gromit opened his eyes to see, not just one Norbot, but a whole chain of Norbots, linking their arms together. One enormous gnome-chain! Before he knew it, Gromit was pulled up the side of the aqueduct and back to safety.

'No job is too small!' said the original Norbot. Gromit hugged him. He had never been so glad to see a gnome!

Wallace was delighted to see the pair getting on so well. 'I knew you'd embrace technology in the end, lad,' he chuckled. He joined them in a group hug. 'Thank goodness you're safe!'

'All right, break it up,' interrupted the

inspector, coming between them. 'This is a crime scene now!'

'Chief!' said PC Mukherjee, trying to get his attention.

'I haven't got time for your apologies, Mukherjee,' said the inspector, impatiently. 'Just arrest Wallace for . . .' He stopped as Mukherjee thrust a pair of binoculars in front of his eyes. 'Flippin' Nora!' he said. 'It IS Feathers McGraw!'

Far away, the small black figure of Feathers could be seen, escaping on the puffing steam train. The penguin held up the diamond bag and waved it at them in triumph.

'AND he's got the diamond!' said a glum PC Mukherjee.

The inspector shook his head, sadly. 'That's ruined my retirement, that has!'

On the steam train, Feathers was feeling very pleased with himself. He'd done it! He'd outwitted them all and got the Blue Diamond for himself. With satisfaction, he reached into the

bag to retrieve the glittering gem. But what he pulled out was – **ANOTHER TURNIP!**

Feathers stared at the root vegetable in disbelief.

Back on the boat, Gromit had a big surprise. Everyone gasped as he held up the Blue Diamond! Good old Gromit! The clever canine had switched the diamond for a turnip, just as Feathers had done all that time ago.

Gromit watched the dejected Feathers departing on the distant train and gave him a triumphant salute.

The inspector couldn't believe his eyes. 'Huh? What?' he stuttered. 'The old turnip switcheroo!'

POLICE

'Cracking move, lad!' said Wallace, with a smile. He couldn't have been prouder.

'Wahay!' shouted the Norbot army.

'I think *you* should have this, Officer,' said Wallace, taking the diamond and presenting it to P. C. Mukherjee.

'Well,' said the inspector, looking much more cheerful. 'Considering what I've just seen, it looks like Mukherjee was right about you being innocent.'

'You mean, I'm not going to jail?' said Wallace, hopefully.

'No,' said the inspector, looking at PC Mukherjee. 'All thanks to the instincts of a fine young copper! You're a natural, Mukherjee!'

'Aw, thanks, Chief,' said Mukherjee, saluting him. 'That means a lot. Happy retirement, sir.' She presented him with the Blue Diamond.

Wallace looked at Gromit with a big grin.

'This is a "turnip" for the books, isn't it, lad!' he chuckled.

Chapter Twenty-three

FRIENDS AGAIN

Mukherjee gave a satisfied sigh as she looked around her new office. Since the chief inspector had retired, she'd been promoted.

She pinned a brand-new **WANTED** poster for Feathers McGraw onto the wall. Finding the fugitive penguin would be a big challenge – but Mukherjee was more than ready for it.

Her retired boss – now known simply as 'Mac' – was happily chugging along the canal on his boat, *Dun Nickin*. It was so peaceful and

relaxing. Suddenly, he leapt up as *Dun Nickin* was overtaken by another craft.

'Oy! Can't you read, Sonny Jim!' he cried. 'Maximum speed **FOUR MILES AN HOUR!**' Mac reached up and stuck a flashing blue light onto the roof of his boat. 'That's three points off your licence for a start!' He chugged off after the offending boat. ***NER NER! NER NER!***

As they say, 'Once a copper, always a copper!'

At 62 West Wallaby Street, Gromit was reading a newspaper with the headline **WALLACE EXONERATED: NOT EVIL INVENTOR – JUST MISUNDERSTOOD**. Wallace came in with a tray of tea and a plate of his favourite cheese and crackers. He was using the old teapot, which had been glued back together again.

'How's my favourite pooch, hm?' he said, putting down the tray. 'Oh – and I've got something for you in the garden.'

Gromit's eyebrows rose in alarm as he looked at his master. Not another of his inventions? He followed Wallace outside, where Norbot was waiting, holding a young sapling in a pot.

'I've upgraded the **PAT-O-MATIC**,' said Wallace, picking up a remote control. Gromit breathed a sigh of relief. At least he couldn't do much harm with that!

Wallace pressed a button. No longer was it the **PAT-O-MATIC** – it was the **PLANT-O-MATIC!**

The upgraded device, now attached to a remote-controlled car, sprang into action. It travelled along and found a planting spot. The mechanical hands quickly dug a hole with a trowel then dropped Norbot's sapling into it. The soil was patted down and Norbot gave it a good watering.

'Da na!' said Norbot as the job was finished. Wallace chuckled and gave Gromit a pat.

'There are some things a machine just can't do,' said Wallace, giving Gromit's ears a good tickle. 'Cheers, me old pal!'

He and Gromit clinked their tea mugs together. Life was good. They'd solved another crime and were delighted to be back to their usual routine. No more crimes, diamonds or evil penguins.

At least – until next time.